MW00976955

Praise for Dawn Van Beck

"Wow! I'm in love... with the short and sweet romances of Debut Author Dawn Van Beck. She's a master storyteller, who makes you feel every bit of the magic in the tales she weaves. Such perfect, little short stories that just make you feel good and offer a wonderful reminder that love triumphs overall. I'm looking forward to her next collection." --- D. D. Scott, International Bestselling Author

Autumn Love

Three Short & Sweet Romance Stories

Dawn Van Beck

First Electronic Edition: September 2019
First Print Edition: October 2019

eBook and Print Book Design & Formatting by
D. D. Scott's LetLoveGlow Author Services

Dedicated to my amazing husband, Jeffrey, who loves me fiercely and is always the true inspiration and hero of all my own love stories.

Table of Contents

Autumn Splendor

"Today we are gathered together to honor the joyous life of Victor Sutton."

Sitting politely on the front row with my parents, I intently listened to Pastor Browning recount numerous facets of my grandfather's full life. PawPaw was strong, active, and joyful to a fault, regardless of his circumstances. Admired by many for his bold confidence, he was never reluctant to go after what he wanted. Anyone who knew him was also familiar with his repetitive mantra, "Never wait or hesitate, or sadly, it might be too late!"

I wish I were more like him.

The room was too quiet. There were no smiles. It reminded me of my horrendous fifteenth birthday party. I loved my PawPaw. I also knew him deeply. Instead of being sad, he would rather we all be celebrating. I breathed an impatient sigh.

Pastor Browning continued, "We come together in grief, acknowledging that love often reveals itself even more deeply in times of loss."

I wondered how much longer the ceremony would last. The air was stuffy, partly due to the large crowd of attendees. The thick odor of old carpet and years of cut flowers didn't help either. At least outside it was a sunny Wisconsin day at the peak of fall.

I stared into the dancing flame of the candle beside the casket, wondering if my life might be different if I, like PawPaw, never waited or hesitated. Perhaps that thought would haunt me for a long time.

My cousin Elliott tapped my shoulder from behind, startling me back to the present moment. He handed me a note. Shame on him.

I opened the note – it wasn't from Elliott. It read, 'Look back to your left'.

Feigning my best nonchalance, I slightly turned, scanning the pews. He nodded at me with a smile. Great. I figured he would show up, but still wasn't prepared to see him…or her. The last thing I needed was to deal with those twisted emotions on top of my PawPaw's passing.

When would this service be over, I wondered. It had been fun and all, but I really needed to scream now.

"Take comfort, knowing heaven will be a place of perpetual reunion."

Finally.

• • •

I busied myself arranging finger sandwiches in the reception hall.

"Hey, Blair!" I turned to discover my friend, Anne, along with five other old friends from Eagle River.

"Hi, you guys. Wow, time flies, eh?"

I'd been back and forth from my hometown in Rockford to PawPaw's cottage several times in the past years, but lost touch with most of the gang after college, except for Anne. We all exchanged hugs and kisses.

"Blair," Anne said, "We're so sorry for your loss. We all loved PawPaw. Hey—did you know Colton's here?"

Oh yeah, I knew, thanks to the little note he'd passed to me in church. It was unnerving, nevertheless touching, that he had driven from Joliet to Eagle River to pay his respects.

"Let's all get together later!" Anne suggested.

Hmmm…a big maybe. I might be too busy. They said goodbye as I went to another table to adjust a few cookie trays. Staring into a tray of almond macaroon fingers, I searched my mind for a good opening line for the inevitable encounter with the man who used to be my very best friend.

"There she is, with her beautiful ginger hair!"

Nothing like a surprise attack. With a deep breath, I turned to face the still-sculpted, ever-handsome Colton Kingsbury.

"It's been a while."

His voice was still sexy. And his black, tousled hair and ice-blue eyes still managed to take my breath away.

"Indeed, it has," I said.

"Come here," he said, pulling me close for a strong embrace. "I'm so sorry. PawPaw was like a grandfather to me. I'm glad to have known him for so many years."

The scent of the woodsy cologne on his neck was arresting.

"Where's Cheryl?" I broke our embrace.

A faint smile crossed Colton's face. "She's not with me."

Good. I'd rather not see her. It made sense—she never even knew PawPaw.

"So...maybe we can hang later?" Colton asked, clearing his throat. "I'd love to talk with you."

I wasn't sure I was up for talking. Things ended rather awkwardly five years ago.

"May I have your attention, please?" My dad's voice over the microphone provided a welcomed interruption.

"On behalf of our family, I'd like to thank you all for coming to share in the joy of knowing my father. For you locals, and those visiting overnight, we'd like to continue our gathering. So, in true PawPaw fashion, we'd like to invite you all to a fish fry at his cabin tonight. We'll provide plenty of fish, but if you're inclined to grab something from the grocery on your way there, we won't object. Hope to see you there."

Sigh. I knew I'd be facing Colton again that evening, and he'd have no clue as to why that would be difficult for me.

The temperature dropped as the crisp, autumn air crowded out the day's sunshine. Donning sweaters and windbreakers, we set up rows of tables into a continuous long line among the Paper Birch trees for one of PawPaw's famous fish fries. A backdrop for our feast was provided by a collection of plump pinecones nestled among the needles of some Red Pines, along with Sugar Maple and Quaking Aspen trees boasting an array of red, orange and yellow leaves. There was enough fresh Perch, Bluegill and Walleye to feed an army, not to mention a plethora of hot side dishes and fruit salads filling the tables.

I missed my PawPaw.

Turned out, it wasn't too bad sitting with Colton and our gang of friends. Sharing great food often lent to warm fellowship. Warm, funny stories emerged about PawPaw, blessing the tables with laughter.

"Remember how PawPaw used to tell us not to go swimming if it's raining because we might get wet?" A wide grin found Anne's face as she spoke.

"Or," I said, "when he took a nap, he'd tell us to wake him up if it's raining, 'cuz he couldn't sleep when it rained!"

"Yeah," Colton chuckled. "And he used to tell us to spit on the worms when we went fishing 'cuz fish liked juicy worms!"

Inhaling the slightly lemony aroma of the stately pines, I beheld the warm smiles around the tables. We reminisced about many fishing trips throughout the chain of lakes, failed water skiing attempts, and Friday night demolition derby races. I recalled the summer I first met Colton; his uncle had a cabin in Eagle River, too—I was twelve years old. Finding out Colton also lived in Rockford was a pleasant bonus.

Conversations were mostly kept to reliving cottage memories, which suited me just fine. I had no desire to hear about what Colton and Cheryl were up to. Admittedly, I was glad to hear they hadn't married yet.

Outdoor lamp posts and individual table lanterns illuminated our faces as stars appeared like scattered moon dust in the sky. The crowd thinned out, tables were cleared, and a crackling fire was started for a circle of stragglers.

"Hey, Colt! We should take the boat out." Two of the guys in our gang egged Colton on to join them for a spin.

Immediate objection flew from my lips as the Benson boys flashed across my mind. The two, wild Benson brothers lived down the road and were notorious for wreaking occasional havoc in the neighborhood. PawPaw used to tell stories of how they'd get drunk and taunt evening bears or race their go-carts around the community's circle drive. One weekend, on a drinking binge, they went out with water skis, swamping area fishing boats, and finished by "streaking" through the channel.

The latest community buzz alerted neighbors of the Benson's new habit of going out on the lake late Saturday nights with their guns. I shuddered to think of Colton and the guys becoming recipients of foolish target practice.

Colton, however, jumped at the opportunity to go out on the lake, and regardless of my concern, my dad granted permission. It was already close to ten o'clock…and it was Saturday night.

"Blair, Colton and the guys will be safe." My dad attempted reassurance. "They're young men now."

• • •

The whistle of the kettle atop the black, antique cook stove summoned me to PawPaw's kitchen. With each step, emerged a loud creak as I walked across the faded linoleum. My parents went to bed, but despite my exhaustion from the day's events, sleep evaded me. The guys were still out on the lake.

Grabbing a wool blanket and my hot mug of tea, I made my way to the screened porch overlooking the channel between two lakes. I settled into PawPaw's favorite shabby chair next to the piano stool that balanced a foot-high stack of magazines, and I waited.

The weight of my eyelids eventually prevailed, and I dozed off, but managed to awaken long enough to see the blurred clock tick past midnight, then again past 12:30. Finally, at about 1 a.m., I was awakened by the idling of the old Evinrude motor.

Colton spotted me under the golden glow of the cast iron wall sconce. He hopped out of the boat and ran up to the porch. "Hey there. Why are you still up? Are you okay?"

"No! I'm not okay. Look how late it is!"

Colton wrinkled his forehead as he rubbed his chin. "Are you mad at me?"

I blinked back tears, hesitating. "No, it's just…so late."

We stared at each other for a long moment before Colton folded his arms in front of him, flashing me a knowing smile.

"Blair Sutton, you were worried about me."

Pursing my lips, I shook my head, frowning. "It's been a long day. I'm going to bed." Gathering my blanket around me, I shuffled inside the cabin without looking back.

As Colton turned to tend to the boat, I heard his faint words, "Good night, beautiful."

I pulled the lace curtains together across the window over the brass bed and plopped down, drawing my grandmother's quilt close. Staring into the dark room, I was relieved Colton was okay, but also furious he continued to see right through me after all these years.

I doubted he discerned I'd fallen in love with him though.

• • •

A gentle tap on my window gradually beckoned me from my slumber. I figured it was a bird. The tapping continued until I finally heard a whisper.

"Wake up, sleepyhead, it's me."

I sat up, pulling open the lace curtains, shielding my eyes from the morning sun.

"Colton, what are you doing?"

"Get dressed. Before I leave shortly, we have to do a lap around the circle drive together…for old time's sake."

I squinted back at Colton, pulling at my sloppy T-shirt.

"C'mon, Blair. I need to talk to you. Besides, I brought you a caramel latte."

My favorite. "Okay, give me a minute. I'll be right out."

I pulled on a shirt and some jeans, brushed my teeth, and grabbed my sweatshirt.

Colton and I walked up the driveway toward the half-mile stretch of pavement circling the neighborhood, with an array of colorful trees inhabiting the center. We sipped our coffee and walked, making small talk, as we spotted a couple of chipmunks and a gray squirrel scavenging for their morning breakfast.

Colton finally heaved a heavy sigh, clearing his throat. "Blair, I'm sorry things got so weird between us after I met Cheryl."

I hesitated a moment before speaking. "I understand, Colton. If I were Cheryl, I wouldn't want to share you, either."

A smile swept across his face.

"So, you go back to Joliet today, eh?" I asked.

"Nope. I go back to Rockford."

A slight chuckle escaped my mouth. "What do you mean?"

"I mean, I moved back there two months ago. That's what I wanted to talk to you about."

My heart skipped a beat as I looked at him, dazed.

"So, you and Cheryl moved back—"

"Blair," Colton said, stopping mid-stride. "When I said yesterday Cheryl wasn't with me, I meant we're no longer together."

Colton continued as we resumed our pace, "It took me a while, but I realized I was never in love with her. I was in love with the idea of her. The most important thing I learned was…she would never be my best friend."

Colton slipped his hand in mine as we continued walking. I swallowed hard, replaying his words in my mind while relishing the warmth of his hand. As we reached the cabin once again, Colton led me out to the end of PawPaw's dock. Leaves of red, gold, and orange gently waved at us from across the channel as the trees reflected across the smooth, still water.

Colton turned to face me, taking both of my hands in his. A strange heat flushed my face as I met his gaze.

"Blair," he said. "PawPaw always said to never wait, or hesitate, so…there's something I need to do."

He pulled me closer as a small cloud of butterflies landed in my stomach.

He cupped my face with both of his hands and whispered, "I've wanted to do this for a long time."

He pressed his lips against mine in a slow, deliberate kiss.

As I leaned my face into his chest in a warm embrace, he gave me a squeeze.

"Blair, am I too late?"

My eyes flickered up to meet his as tears blurred my vision.

Wrapping my arms around his neck, I pulled his face to mine…and kissed him right back.

As the Leaves Turn

"If you have the time, Mackinac Island is a must-see."

He stood at the edge of the bench on the boardwalk, his hands in the pockets of his white, Bermuda shorts. Turning around from her spot, she paused, not quite sure how to react to the man standing behind her.

"Excuse me?"

"I just thought I'd give you some sightseeing advice."

She chuckled, realizing he'd caught sight of her brochure.

"Am I that obvious?" She dropped her hands to her lap as he walked around to the front of the bench.

"Well, you did have a brochure completely spread out in front of you, titled, 'Things to Do in St. Ignace'."

"Busted. Yes, I'm a tourist." She positioned the bridge of her sunglasses snug against her face, breathing in the crisp, fresh smell of the lake waters.

"In that case, welcome. My name's Brandon. Brandon Walker."

She cleared her throat, without providing her name. "So, I've always been under the impression that the north woods of Michigan's upper peninsula were off the grid, but it seems pretty crowded here."

Brandon removed his hands from his pockets and clapped them together, looking out toward the marina. "That's because you're here in July. You need to visit in October. The same sights and excursions are available then, but without all the hustle and bustle."

Brandon dropped his arms to his sides, turning to face her. He flashed her a gentle smile, revealing a pronounced dimple.

"There's nothing like St. Ignace in the Fall," he said.

Her thoughts became scrambled by his well-defined physique. His brown, loose curls resting below his ears gently swayed in the summer breeze as his five o'clock shadow accented his face. She felt a mild heat fill her cheeks as she stole a quick breath.

"So, my name's Grace. I'm just here for a brief visit. Mackinac Island, you say? How do I get there?"

Brandon shoved his hands back in his pockets. "There's ferry boats running continuously every day. Or, I could take you tomorrow morning."

"What? Don't you think that's a bit presumptuous?" Her voice slightly cracked with shock.

Brandon lowered his sunglasses slightly to reveal velvet, brown eyes, and held her gaze with a knowing smile.

"Um…no. I meant, I could take you there in my boat. I run a charter fishing business. I just thought it might be a nice alternative to the mass of people who'll be sharing the ferry, that's all."

"Oh, of course." She looked down and tugged at the sides of her flouncy, white blouse. "So, you don't have a fishing charter tomorrow?"

"Nope."

Grace scraped her hand through her long strands of blonde hair.

"Well, I'll probably just take the ferry." Her eyes flickered up to meet his.

"Suit yourself. It's nice meeting you, Grace. I gotta go, or I'll be late."

Brandon made a slight bow toward her and gave a mild salute before he began walking down the boardwalk. She turned to watch him leave.

"Late for what?" she called out, her curiosity surprising her.

Brandon turned on his heels and shouted back, "My other job."

Grace left the boardwalk and walked back to her hotel. From her second-floor balcony, she watched a gaggle of geese darting along the sandy shore. She looked out at the crystal, clear waters of Lake Huron, questioning everything about her life she thought to be true, and wondering why she couldn't stop thinking about Brandon.

• • •

Grace's sandals slapped the wood of the boardwalk as she made her way to the marina the next morning. Approaching the docks, she was overcome by the noxious vapors of oil and gas as several boats chugged in idle, awaiting the day's activity. She located the Mackinac Island ferry boat, stopping behind the flock of people huddled near the entrance, waiting to board. She heaved a heavy sigh, recalling Brandon's accurate reference to the mass of people.

"Morning to ya!"

The jovial voice to her left came from a power boat. Turning toward the boat, the sight of the sculpted man standing on board wearing a Detroit Tigers hat, denim jeans, and no shirt made her heart skip a beat. Brandon.

"Oh, hey." She pulled her small backpack tighter to her shoulder.

Brandon put a long-sleeved shirt on, keeping it open in the front. Picking up a rag, he began wiping his hands, noting how cute Grace appeared in her khaki shorts, coral tank top and her floral ball cap.

"My offer's still good if you're reconsidering about the ferry boat."

Grace glanced over to the crowd of tourists lined up on the dock, complete with several young children and a crying baby. She bit her lower lip, as the air horn blasted on the ferry.

"Um, sure."

"Great. It's just about a twenty-minute ride. I'll take you under the mighty Mackinac Bridge first, then the island. I'll show you around when we get there, if you'd like."

"Okay, I guess." Grace nodded with a tight expression, rubbing the back of her neck.

Brandon reached out to help her inside the boat, creating a mild flutter in her chest at the touch of his hand. She settled into the chair opposite the driver's seat, clutching her backpack. The boat sped forward and began to glide through the water, splicing the oncoming waves. She looked out onto the horizon, and with a deep breath, declared herself to be completely mad.

While Brandon finally secured the boat to the dock, Grace looked ahead of her on the island. Brandon followed her line of vision.

"Not too crowded yet, but just wait. It'll be packed in a couple of hours. I need another cup of coffee. There's a great little coffee shop around the corner. C'mon."

Brandon led her to a quaint shop around the corner, decorated with wood pallet walls and hanging barn lights.

"How do you like your coffee?" He motioned for her to sit across from him.

"Um, you know this is not a date, right?"

Brandon chuckled. "Um, and you know this is just a cup of coffee, right? So, why don't you tell me what brought you to St. Ignace?"

They gave their orders to the waitress. Brandon leaned back in his chair, arms folded in front, as Grace provided a bit of personal history. She told him she lived in Chicago, had grown up there, and always wanted to attend one of the summer workshops at the Crooked Tree Arts Center in Traverse City. So, she finally did.

Brandon noted her sky-blue eyes sparkled when she spoke about art.

"My three-day workshop was called, 'Winning with Watercolor'. I loved it…learned a lot. Then, I thought since I was so close, I'd check out St. Ignace for a day."

"So, you're an artist. Impressive."

Grace felt a flush across her cheeks. No one had ever referred to her as an artist. She went on to clarify she worked as a gallery assistant, though she hoped to one day have her own work displayed.

"You know they have an artist in residence program right here in St. Ignace?"

"Really?" Grace was a bit taken aback. "No, I didn't know that."

"Did I hear you say you're only here until tomorrow?"

She nodded.

"Then, we'd better make the most of our day."

She studied Brandon as he began dispensing facts about Mackinac Island and its history. He seemed confident and comfortable all the time, which she envied. When the coffee arrived, it was a relief to have something to busy her jittery hands. She sipped her cappuccino in silence as Brandon continued his verbal tour guiding.

He explained the only access to the island was by boat or small plane and that no motorized vehicles were allowed except for service vehicles. The island hosted the famed Grand Hotel, old historic buildings, museums, and specialty shops.

"There's lots of ways to enjoy the island." Brandon took a large gulp of his black coffee. "You can bicycle, ride a horse, hike, enjoy a horse drawn carriage, or walk."

Grace straightened up in her chair, folding her hands in front of her.

"Brandon," she said, clearing her throat. "Since we're going to be spending the day together, I think you should know I have a boyfriend back home. In fact, we're almost engaged."

"Okay…that's great. I am curious, though…how can one be 'almost' engaged?"

"Well," she said, tapping her coffee mug, "I just mean we've been together a long time, and we'll probably be engaged soon."

"Ah, but he hasn't proposed yet?"

"No." Grace suddenly felt foolish. "You don't understand. Trust me, it's in our plans to marry. Eventually."

"Of course." Brandon leaned forward. "So, does this almost fiancé have a name?"

"Dexter."

Brandon held her gaze for a moment, flashing a weak smile that made her shift in her chair.

"So, tell me a bit about Dexter, your future husband."

Grace explained that Dexter worked downtown as an insurance adjustor. His parents lived in Lincoln Park."

"Lincoln Park, eh?" Brandon interrupted with a mild chuckle. "So then, you must be marrying for money."

"No, no. Not at all." Grace protested. "He's just…nice, you know?"

No, Brandon didn't know, but he figured it didn't matter. It wasn't any of his business.

Grace went on to say how Dexter worked long hours – sometimes too long – and when he wasn't working, he was working out.

"How about you?" Brandon asked. "You're obviously in great shape. You must be a fitness guru, too." Grace's slender curves had not gone unnoticed.

“Well,” she said, “I stay in shape and all, but I don’t work at it nearly as much as Dexter would like me to. I just don’t see the point.”

Brandon looked away, slightly rolling his eyes.

“What about you? Is there a special girl you’re dating right now?

Brandon chuckled, shaking his head. “Nope. Not currently dating and not planning on ever dating again.”

“Never again?” Grace wrinkled her forehead. “You wish to be alone the rest of your life?”

“Oh no, not at all. I just don’t believe in the whole dating scene…it’s a waste of precious time and energy. I just think if two people know they want to be together, then…they should just be together.”

“I see,” Grace said, setting her jaw in a smirk. “You’re pretty direct. Don’t you think it’s a bit more complicated than that?”

Brandon looked upward, pausing to collect his thoughts. “Not really. Think about it. Wouldn’t you agree that most people know rather quickly if they’d like to be with someone?”

With a sudden blush, Grace stared down at her coffee mug.

“Well, we should get started on our island adventure,” Brandon said, feeling bad he’d made her uncomfortable. “The best way to experience the island’s beauty is by tandem bicycle. It’s eight miles around the entire island. C’mon, you can tell ‘Dex’ you got your exercise for the day.”

• • •

If anything could forcibly bring two people closer together, it's a long tandem bike ride.

For a smooth ride and to prevent crashing onto the side of the road, it was imperative for Grace and Brandon to communicate with each other. They had to learn how to move together, to sense each other's rhythms, and speak up when either one needed to change pace. Following a bumpy beginning, which included Grace suffering a nasty bite from a horse fly, they finally fell into a groove and, with every mile, became increasingly more comfortable with each other.

Their conversation began to flow freely, too, as Grace bubbled about her love of art and how she'd participated in sidewalk chalk events and downtown paint-outs, hoping to somehow get noticed. Brandon talked about the few fishermen, such as himself, who stay in St. Ignace year-round, finding it necessary to do odds jobs during the brutal winters, and despite the brutality of the season, how beautiful the lake was when completely frozen.

"This island is beautiful, Brandon. So, when did you move to St. Ignace?" Grace asked.

"Born and raised here."

"No kidding?" Grace's eyes widened.

"Yep. My dad owned and operated a fish hatchery, so, many days, I was out on the water before the sun came up, and often long after the sun went down."

"So," Grace continued, "what was your reason for staying?"

Brandon pedaled in silence for a long moment before answering. "I never saw any good reason to leave."

A faint smile crossed Grace's face as she reflected on how nice it must be to be completely content with where you are.

Upon finishing the eight-mile trek, their stomachs signaled a necessary lunch break. Brandon led the way to the island's Bridge Side Bistro, which provided a bird's eye view of the lake with Mackinac Bridge towering in the distance.

As they made their way to a table, Brandon noted the sweet, vanilla musk that laid down a light track wherever Grace walked. Sitting before her, a faint smile swept across his face as he took in her loose-braided, long pigtails with wisps of stray hairs on both sides framing her soft face.

Feeling his eyes on her, a slight heat rushed to Grace's cheeks.

"Well," she said, breaking the moment, "I'm starved. Everything on the menu looks great!"

When the waitress arrived, Grace wasted no time, "I'll have the arugula salad with candied pecans, green apple and blue cheese." She snapped her menu shut and handed it over to their waitress.

"See?" Brandon flashed a wide grin. "You can be decisive."

He calmly folded his menu, nodding at the waitress as he handed it to her. "I'll have the grilled avocado tapas with the roasted tomato salsa. Thank you."

Brandon's confident ease made Grace slightly uncomfortable. And, what did he mean by his comment about her being able to make a decision? With a short breath, she set her shoulders back, attempting to dismiss her thoughts.

"Please excuse me, Brandon." On second thought, perhaps a brief change of scenery would be helpful. "I'm going to freshen up...I'll be right back."

"Sure."

As she stood, Brandon caught sight of the half-exposed sketch pad emerging from her backpack.

"Grace...may I?"

Grace followed his line of vision to her sketch pad. "Go ahead." She shrugged her shoulders, biting her lower lip. "I'm afraid there's not much to see."

She handed him the pad and set out for the ladies' room.

Brandon took a sip of water, sat back in his chair, and began surveying the thick, bound pages boasting an array of detailed drawings, coming to life with each turn of the page. A rustic cabin nestled in the woods by a lake, a still life painting of a blue, artisanal vase housing an arrangement of wildflowers, sketches of children's faces held in laughter, a beautiful young woman with flowing, long hair…with a tear rolling down her cheek. Brandon leaned in toward each page, slowly shaking his head.

Upon her return, he gently handed the sketch pad back to her and just stared.

Her eyes narrowed. "What's the matter?" She asked.

"Grace," Brandon said, leaning toward her, sliding his chair closer to the table, "your work is really good."

Grace waved him off as she shuffled her feet beneath her.

"No, really. I'm serious. Your attention to minute detail, your exquisite shading techniques…you're very talented." He leaned back in his chair, folding his arms in front of him. "Dex must be so proud."

Grace swallowed hard. She'd never heard such affirming words from Dexter.

"Well, it's not really his cup of tea. But that's okay." Was it? She suddenly wondered.

Their food orders arrived, and they began eating in awkward silence; well, it was awkward for Grace.

"So, do you like the city life, then?" Finally, Brandon broke their silence with another one of his many questions.

Grace finished chewing her bit of food before answering, "It's not my first choice of where I'd love to live. I mean, to be honest, I grow tired of my scenery mostly consisting of steam exhaling through manhole covers, but it's okay." As soon as her words left her lips, she regretted having spoken them.

"So, why would you live there if you don't love it?"

Grace raised an eyebrow.

Brandon raised one right back. "Ah, of course. Dex."

Brandon slowly tilted his head to the side, pausing to examine her.

As she looked at him, she suddenly felt as if his eyes were penetrating her very soul. At that moment, she wanted him to eat his food. Sing. Shout. Anything but look at her the way he was.

Her brow furrowed as if she were working through a puzzle that only she could see.

"You obviously have something to say, Brandon. What is it?"

Brandon looked down, finishing the last bite of his lunch. Without looking up, he spoke with a gentle tone, "Grace, you're beautiful, talented, sexy, and fun. It just surprises me you're so willing to compromise on things that mean a lot to you. In my book, relationships are all about accepting each other for who they are and celebrating that. I just wonder if Dex is celebrating you, that's all."

Speechless, Grace pushed her finished plate forward as her eyes brimmed with tears.

"Oh, Grace, I'm so sorry. Sometimes, I don't know when to keep my mouth shut. I was clearly out of line. I didn't mean to upset you." Brandon reached forward and squeezed her hand resting on the table. "I'm sorry. C'mon, you must see the rest of the island before you leave tomorrow. Let me show you the museum and a few shops before I take you back, okay? I promise I won't talk, like, at all!"

A faint smile crossed Grace's face as she rose to her feet and nodded.

• • •

Contrary to Brandon's promise, he continued to talk throughout the rest of the afternoon. Grace had the distinct suspicion he was doing so to ease her tension, which she gladly allowed. He pointed out historical facts about St. Ignace at the museum. As they browsed gift shops, he talked about ice fishing and snowmobile racing. As they stopped for an ice cream break, he told her all about the immense beauty of the Hiawatha National Forest, reminding her once again there was nothing like St. Ignace in the Fall.

Grace really wasn't upset that he spoke his mind earlier. She was more upset about the gnawing churning in her gut she was now feeling, questioning the extent of which his words may be true.

By late afternoon, many tourists had left the island, leaving room for evening dinner crowds and horse-drawn buggy rides. Grace could still smell the clean sandalwood of Brandon's cologne as he took her hand and led her back into the boat. Caressed by a gentle, warm breeze, she watched the fading sun cut a ribbon across the waves on the lake, while Brandon's words reverberated in her mind.

"Thank you for a lovely day." Grace pulled the strap of her backpack over her shoulder as she stood on the boardwalk.

Brandon finished tying down the boat and hopped off the dock to join her. He stood before her, removing his hat.

"The pleasure was truly all mine. Grace," he said and paused. "I don't want your visit to end on a bad note. So, as my way of apologizing, once again, for making you feel uncomfortable earlier, I'd like to treat you to dinner."

"Oh, I don't think so," Grace said, looking upward and shaking her head.

"No, you don't understand. I'd like to treat you to dinner, but not with me. I won't be there. I'm working tonight, anyway. It's just, well, I personally know the chef at what's heralded as the best sports bar in the area. You'll not enjoy a better, more authentic meal anywhere else. Just show up anytime this evening, and I'll make sure you're well taken care of."

Grace pressed her lips into a fine line of anxiety. "Oh, I don't know."

"Honestly, Grace. You can't say you've truly been in St. Ignace until you've tried some fresh Whitefish, or Yellow Lake Perch. Here's a card for the Dockside Sports Bar. It's just down there, across the street. Enjoy yourself. Oh, and have a safe trip home."

With that, Brandon turned on his heels and walked away. Just like that.

• • •

Grace meandered down the road for three blocks until she reached her hotel. Upon entering her room, she tossed her backpack on the bed and opened the sliding door to encourage a lake breeze. As she sat on her balcony overlooking Lake Huron, she breathed in the smell of fresh wind and lemons and pondered if she should go to the Dockside for dinner. She probably should. After all, it was such a kind gesture, and Brandon would probably find out if she refused his offer. She certainly didn't want to hurt his feelings.

Studying the clarity and patterns of the sandstone around the edge of the water before her, thoughts of him consumed her mind. Brandon. He was a good man. Handsome, strong, confident, funny…kind. He easily brought her to laughter. He made her feel good about herself. When he held her gaze, she could feel her palms sweat. And his smile? Well, his smile made her heart thunder.

In the process of trying to decipher the effects Brandon seemed to have on her, Grace made a stark realization. Dexter hadn't called her once. She also realized that she almost hadn't noticed.

She showered and put on a simple sundress, adding a light touch of makeup. Making her way to the Dockside, she couldn't ignore the strange quivers in her stomach.

• • •

"You must be Grace." A waitress greeted her inside the door.

"How did you know?"

"That's easy," the waitress said and smiled. "Your beautiful hair, of course. Right this way."

The waitress ushered Grace to a seat by a window overlooking the boardwalk, the smell of cooked fish wafting in the air. Glancing out at the marina, she chuckled, knowing the comment about her hair could only have come from Brandon. The Dockside was a general sports bar, however, judging by many of the pictures on the wall and various memorabilia, there was a definite affinity for baseball. The overhead televisions hummed a game between the Orioles and Angels as she studied the menu and sipped some water. Hmmm. Yellow Lake Perch, deep fried with fries, or, fresh, Great Lakes Whitefish baked on a maple wood plank surrounded with duchess potatoes and a vegetable.

As the waitress approached, Grace slapped her menu on the high-top table. "I'll definitely have the Whitefish."

"Excellent. There's a woman who knows how to make a decision! You won't be disappointed. It's delicious. Our chef is the best around."

"So, I've heard."

Brandon's comment from earlier that day suddenly flashed across Grace's mind. So, you can be decisive. That's what he'd said. A deep breath escaped her lungs as she frowned. She was certainly proficient in deciding on menu choices, but perhaps not as skilled at deciding anything else in her life.

She enjoyed a delicious meal as she watched boats coming and going from the marina across the street. The sun began to fall behind the horizon, painting the sky shades of pink and red. Ice clinked gently in her glass as she wondered what Brandon was doing at that moment. Where was his other job? Perhaps, if she took an evening walk around her surrounding territory, she might find out and run into him. Then again, what would be the purpose of that? She was leaving tomorrow morning…never to see him again.

"Are you finished here?" The waitress asked, breaking her concentration.

"Oh, yes. Thank you. It was delicious. This has been such a treat. Would it be possible for me to thank the chef in person?"

"Why, of course. I'll send him out." The waitress gathered up most of the dishes and started to turn toward the kitchen.

"So, I have to ask," Grace said, stopping her. "Do you, by any chance, know Brandon Walker?"

The waitress paused, squinting her eyes with a smirk. "Honey, everyone knows Brandon."

The waitress disappeared into the kitchen. Grace folded and smoothed her napkin on the table, continuing to watch the sunset. Just as she folded her hands, resting them in her lap, she felt a gentle tap on her shoulder. She turned to her side to see none other than Brandon standing before her. He was wearing a chef's hat.

"You wanted to see me?" He flashed a generous smile.

Grace's mouth dropped open. "Well, I'll be. This is your other job?"

"Afraid so. I've found that the second-best thing to catching fish is cooking them."

"I'm so surprised." Grace brought her hand to her chest. "It was delectable. Brandon, you continually amaze me."

"Hope so."

"Well, I'd really like to reward your exquisite work and pay for my meal."

"Not possible. It's my treat." Brandon brought his heels together and nodded. "Compliments of the chef."

"Very well then, thank you. I guess I'd better get going. I've got an early start tomorrow morning." She rose from her chair, retrieving her small purse.

Brandon noted how her long, silky hair fell around her like a curtain.

She turned to face him. "Mr. Brandon Walker, thank you…for everything."

As she took a step to leave, Brandon stopped her. "Grace, will I see you again?"

The air closed in around her throat as she held his gaze. How could she answer that? She couldn't deny the thought of returning to St. Ignace had crossed her mind, but her mind still searched for a logical reason for her thoughts.

Brandon searched her face with pensive eyes.

"Grace, please tell me I'm not as forgettable as your silence is making me feel."

Although he stood inches away from her, she could feel a line of heat between them as if they were touching.

"Brandon, of course not. I mean, you're great. How could anyone forget you? It's just…I don't know how to answer that question." She dropped her gaze to the floor. "I'm sorry."

Brandon clapped his hands together, lightening his tone, "Hey, no worries. I didn't mean to make you uncomfortable. Listen, it's been a true pleasure getting to know you. I wish you the very best."

Without hesitation, he pulled her to him and held her in a warm embrace.

Lost in the moment, she stretched her arms around him, feeling the muscles of his back. Finally, she stepped back, breaking their hug.

"I gotta go." She smiled a soft smile, pulled her purse around her shoulder, and walked out the door.

Brandon removed the water carafe from her table, breathing in the sweet scent of her delicate perfume still hanging in the air. As he glanced out the window, he caught glimpse of her crossing the street and a sudden tightness filled his chest. A feeling he suspected wouldn't be going away anytime soon.

• • •

Darkness hugged the sky on Grace's brisk walk back to her hotel. Upon entering her room, she busied herself as much as possible. She packed her belongings, organized her purse, vigorously brushed her hair, and turned the television on, just for chatter. She was determined to think of anything else besides the strong, warm arms of Brandon Walker.

She rose early the next morning, after a restless night of sleep. Checking out at the front desk, she brought her suitcase and backpack out to her car. As she slammed the trunk of the car shut, she felt as though someone was watching her. She slowly turned to the guttural, thrumming sound of an idling motorcycle. Brandon.

At the edge of the hotel parking lot, near the road, sat Brandon on a motorcycle, his arms folded in front of him. No motions were made, no words were spoken. They just...stared. Finally, he flashed her his killer smile, retrieving his helmet from the handlebar. After fastening the straps, he gently waved, revved his engine, and cruised down the road out of sight.

Grace set out on the road for the six and one-half hour drive back to Chicago, irritated. Why did he show up like that? His presence just messed with her already-confused mind. But then she wondered why she felt confused in the first place. Erratic thoughts flew wildly around her head, like a trapped parakeet in a closed room. She turned her attention to thoughts of Dexter, examining him the entire drive home.

Did he support her artwork and her dreams? Would he always want her to be more athletic? Why did he sometimes make her feel as though she annoyed him? Would he ever want to move away from a big city? Was he happy with her? Was she happy with him?

A sharp ache stung her chest as she asked herself one final question...

Was Dexter her lighthouse, or was he the storm?

• • •

Crimson leaves crunched beneath Grace's feet before she walked inside the room and found a place to sit. Her knee bounced up and down as she opened the Dockside menu, then snapped it shut again. She already knew what she wanted. In fact, she could hardly contain her excitement. She felt like a kindergartner on her first day of school…not exactly sure what to expect but anticipating it would be something good. Her fingers flexed to the beat of her racing pulse.

"I'll have the Whitefish," she blurted out her order before the waitress even had a chance to greet her.

The waitress smiled, perplexed.

"I'm so sorry. It's just, well, I know what I want!" Grace took a deep breath and cleared her throat. "Also, can you tell Brandon that Grace is here?"

"Who?" The waitress's head flinched back slightly. "Um, I'm pretty new here, so I don't know who Brandon is."

"Oh, that's okay." Grace folded her hands together. "Just tell them in the kitchen. They'll know who I'm talking about."

"You got it." The waitress disappeared around the corner.

Grace took in a long breath as she glanced out at the marina. The brisk breeze sent orange and yellow leaves tumbling through the air. She closed her eyes and took a long, calming breath.

"Excuse me, ma'am?" The waitress interrupted her thoughts. "I'm sorry, but there's no Brandon here."

"What?!" Grace's thoughts swirled. Where was he? Was it his night off? Did he still work there? Was he still in St. Ignace? Where was he?

Flustered, she fidgeted with her fingers while tapping her foot. A sudden, empty feeling filled the pit of her stomach. She breathed in hard through her nose and looked up at the waitress.

"On second thought, I think I'll pass on dinner. Thank you anyway."

Grace couldn't get out of the restaurant fast enough. Walking to the marina, she surveyed the anchored boats, looking for Brandon's. Many of them looked alike, and she hadn't paid close enough attention three months ago. What if she couldn't find him?

She aimlessly wandered up and down the main street of St. Ignace, pulling her coat snug around her body as the brisk evening breeze began to bite. The aroma of smoked spareribs poured out from a nearby barbecue shack, and the gift shop windows all displayed arrays of fall decorations, autumn knickknacks, and winter clothing. She walked for what seemed like hours before returning to her hotel.

"Excuse me, Miss Montgomery?" The clerk stopped her as she passed by the front desk.

"Yes? That's me."

"I have a message for you, ma'am. Right here."

The clerk handed her a light blue envelope with her first name written on the front, along with a solitary, yellow rose. She politely thanked the clerk before dashing around the corner near the elevator to open the envelope. The message was short and to the point:

Grace,

I'm so glad you're here. Meet me tomorrow morning at 9:00 a.m. at the first parking lot of the Hiawatha National Forest, near the Roaring Fork trail head.

Fondly,
Brandon

So, maybe he hadn't been at the Dockside, but someone obviously got word to him that she was here. Grace lay in her hotel bed that night in pitch darkness. She stared at the dark ceiling above her, gently tapping her fingers on the bedspread, wondering, what now?

Directing her car onto the gravel parking lot, she took in the sight of brilliantly colored leaves against an azure, morning sky. His motorcycle was parked at the far corner. Stepping out of her car into the crisp, invigorating air, she tightened her hiking boots and zipped up her jacket, scanning the front edge of the trail heads. Roaring Fork. Taking a few steps forward, she spotted the sign. But where was Brandon?

With a sudden lurch in her stomach, she began walking forward onto the Roaring Fork path. When she spotted his handsome physique wearing dark blue jeans, a gray quarter-zip wool sweater, and a bright blue shirt underneath, coming at her from the opposite direction, her heart thumped against her chest.

"You found me." He flashed her a wide grin, walking toward her.

Yes, she thought. I found you. A tingling in her chest signaled her mild disbelief that she was there in the north woods of Michigan's upper peninsula, once again, with Brandon.

"So, why did you make me come out here?" Grace opened her hands as they continued walking toward each other.

"I wanted to see if you would really show up."

"Oh, Brandon, I need to say something." Her heart raced. "I've come all this way. I need to tell you why I'm here."

They finally caught up to each other and, without hesitation, Brandon enveloped her in a big hug.

"Shhhhhhh." Brandon put his finger to her lips. "Come with me."

He boldly took her hand as they set out on a mild hike toward the lake.

"Keep your eyes open. Some of the best wilderness is found off the coastline outside of Lake Huron."

The earthy smell of the damp ground combined with fallen leaves had a calming effect as they walked together on a trail lined with large clusters of honeysuckle bushes, still boasting their hardy leaves. The surrounding trees paraded leaves of vivid orange, plum, and gold colors, breathtaking amid the crisp, autumn morning. The sweet smell of pine permeated the air as they finally reached the outskirts of the lake.

"Okay, here we are." Brandon dropped Grace's hand. "Now, we're looking for a specific tree along the shoreline with a profound, crooked branch."

"What are you talking about?" Grace squished her eyebrows together. "Brandon, I really want to tell you why I'm here."

"In a minute, I promise. Bear with me. Help me find that tree."

Grace pressed her lips into a fine line as intermittent brushes of lake mist tickled her cheeks. They both walked a few steps in different directions, searching for the crooked tree. Grace stumbled upon a stately maple tree whose leaves had transformed into a brilliant red. A large, sturdy branch protruded off to the side of the tree, extending sideways.

"I think I found it!" She squealed.

"Yep, that's it. Nice work." Brandon rushed over to where she was standing. "Now, please be patient for just one more minute."

"But Brandon," she began to plead.

"Grace," he interrupted her. "One more minute, I promise. Then, we will talk."

Grace stood back, folding her arms in front of her as she watched Brandon begin to dig up a small hole underneath the beginning section of the crooked branch. As perplexed as she was, she knew it would do no good to demand an explanation in that moment.

He finally stopped, pulling forth a small, tin box from the earth. She leaned forward, edging closer to Brandon and the box. Brushing dirt and twigs off the top, he stood before her with the box in his hands.

"What in the world is this?" She wrinkled her nose.

"Well," he began to explain, "in this box is something I've wanted to share with you for three months."

"How did you know I'd come back?"

"I didn't," he said. "Grace, tell me now. Why did you come back?"

"Oh, Brandon," she said. "I…I…well, I finally made some decisions in my life, and well…oh, good grief!" Her heart fluttered as her words jumbled together, attempting to explain herself while fighting off the collision of emotions overwhelming her. Finally, she released a heavy sigh and met Brandon's gaze, a soft smile filling her face. "Brandon, I've come to an important realization."

"I'm dying to know. What is it?" He narrowed his eyes, focusing intently on her.

"I've made a significant discovery." A slight chuckled escaped her lips. "The thing is, Brandon…I've come to realize that you are the lighthouse rather than the storm."

Brandon pressed his lips together in a hard, obvious swallow.

"And," she continued, "I've been waiting for three months for you to kiss me."

A wide grin crossed his face as he began to open the small, tin box.

"Good things come to those who wait, Grace."

Once the box was open, Brandon pulled out a yellow piece of paper, folded up into a small square. Putting the box on the ground, he carefully unfolded it, holding it open.

Grace clutched her hands together in eager anticipation. Brandon took one of her hands, intertwining his fingers with hers. Blowing out a long breath, he smiled before he read the contents of the yellow piece of paper.

Beautiful Grace,

Come back to me and you will see
That you've become a part of me
You're in my thoughts and prayers each day
And I've been empty since you went away
I know you're not like all the rest
You're a fine treasure
With you, I'm blessed
So, come back to me and you will see
That you and I are meant to be

His gaze was steady as he took her hands in his. Her eyes wrinkled with pleasure as she blinked back tears.

"Now," he said, "I don't think we should wait any longer."

The world around her suddenly fell away as Brandon pulled her closer to him.

As he gently guided her long strands of hair away from her face, he breathed in the sweet fragrance of her familiar perfume. He framed her face with his palms, a light breeze tickling the leaves around them. He leaned in and began kissing her soft lips.

Grace returned his kiss with an eagerness that made her head spin.

She savored the woodsy aroma of his sweater as they relaxed in a warm embrace. Interlocked at their sides, they walked down to the water's edge, looking out at the fresh, choppy lake waters.

"You were right, you know." Grace squeezed Brandon's side as he put his arm around her.

"Oh yeah? About what?"

Grace leaned forward, stealing another kiss, her eyes beaming. "There's nothing like St. Ignace in the Fall."

VICTORIAN FALL

Leaning forward at the side of her bed, Kendall reminded himself to obey the doctor's directions and refrain from touching her.

Cold, lifeless eyes met his gaze amid the sterile odor of antiseptic permeating the room.

"Jasmine, baby. You're at Mercy Hospital. It was a bad accident. You were temporarily unconscious, but you're okay."

Jasmine's eyes narrowed. "Why did you call me 'baby'?"

Kendall stood erect, his head jerking back. He searched Jasmine's face as the doctor stood in the back corner of the room.

"What do you mean?" Kendall recalled how inseparable they'd been for the past two years as the memory of her soft voice rang in the corridors of his heart.

"My God, Jasmine. You don't know who I am, do you? It's me…Kendall."

On instinct, he reached out his hand toward her face, causing her to flinch. Stepping back, he turned toward the doctor with wild eyes. The doctor motioned him to the back of the room.

"Kendall, as we suspected, your girlfriend has amnesia…caused by her head injury."

The air evaporated from Kendall's lungs and tears blurred his vision as he turned to face Jasmine. "Everything will be all right, Jasmine. You'll get better, I promise."

Darting down the hall, he flung himself into a chair in the waiting room. He sat, running his fingers through his hair. Upon finding him, the doctor sat beside him, placing his hand on Kendall's shoulder.

"Stay positive, son. We don't know how long this may last. The best you can do right now is visit frequently and keep talking to her. Discuss details of your lives. Events you've shared. Things that may trigger her memory. Be careful though. This may take time. Don't push her, or she might not wish to see you, at all."

Kendall nodded and remained in the dark waiting room until the next morning.

Rising from his chair, he squinted at the light beaming in through the blinds. Stretching his arms, he located a coffee machine. With coffee in one hand, he rubbed the back of his neck with the other and approached Jasmine's room.

He watched the nurse adjust her monitor. "May I speak with her?"

"Certainly," the nurse said. "I'm all done. Push the red button if you need anything."

Jasmine, awake and alert, studied Kendall as he pulled up a chair, positioning it beside her bed. He swallowed hard, hesitating.

"I don't want to upset you," he said, his voice gentle. "I just want to talk."

Jasmine's eyes sparkled as she smiled. "I know. I don't believe you mean any harm."

Kendall released a breath he didn't know he was holding, relieved her infectious smile had found him.

"Has anyone explained what happened to you?" He asked.

"Not in detail." Jasmine licked her chapped lips. "There's a lot of pain though."

"Yeah, so…let's start there."

Kendall began explaining the events of Jasmine's crash. She was driving home from work. A truck made a wide turn and didn't see her approaching. It was a head-on collision. She suffered multiple fractures, including a fractured pelvis and blunt trauma to her head.

"That explains this fashionable gauze headdress I'm sporting, right?" She asked.

Kendall chuckled, a spark of hope emerging from hearing her familiar sense of humor. "Yes, actually. And just so you know, your headpiece is hiding an adorable brunette, pixie haircut."

Jasmine stared at him with no response.

"Anyway," Kendall continued, but not until after he swallowed hard at the thought of her perceiving him as a total stranger.

He told her it was March. Possessing a fierce passion for reading, she worked in a bookstore in Downtown Baltimore. He told her all about her love of jazz, her insatiable affinity for popcorn, and her rooftop apartment boasting a balcony brimming with plants.

As Kendall's hospital visits continued over the next two months, he tried to recount special occasions, silly moments – anything in Jasmine's life that might trigger her remembrance, all the while keeping sensitive to each subject he brought up with her. Forced to measure every word he spoke, barbs of pain stabbed at his chest.

They were crazy in love...how could she not remember?

"Tell me about you," she said one afternoon.

Surprised by this new inquiry, Kendall obliged without hesitation. "Well, let's see," he began, "I'm a graphic designer with a strong aversion to any species of spiders. I bike every morning, regardless of the weather. I loathe injustice of any kind, and I make a mean chicken enchilada."

Although Kendall's playful tone still managed to evoke giggles from Jasmine, each memory he shared was met by her vacant eyes.

C'mon, Jazzie...remember!

• • •

Since Jasmine's transfer to a rehab facility, renewed hope held Kendall's thoughts captive. Her next step of recovery was underway.

On a sunny day in June, he set down a vase of fresh-cut flowers on her tray table. Jasmine tapped her fingers incessantly as Kendall rambled about current events. She didn't care about the local news, evidently. She wanted to know more about other things.

"Will you tell me about us?" She interrupted him.

Kendall paused, measuring his words. "Certainly. Maybe it will help."

Kendall told her how they met in the bookstore where she worked. They went out for breakfast every Saturday morning. They enjoyed sitting on her rooftop at night, watching the stars dot the sky. They'd been together a little over two years now. And they were crazy in love.

He halted, finally knowing exactly what to share – Cape May, New Jersey. There was nothing like a Victorian Fall.

"Eight months ago, we took a trip to Cape May. Remember the lighthouse overlooking Delaware Bay?" He asked.

She frowned, shaking her head.

He recounted their October trip, when they attended the Victorian Weekend Festival. They each dressed in Victorian costumes to attend the annual festival comprised of Victorian parlor games, historic tours, trolley rides, crafts and more. The highlight of their weekend was climbing the 199 steps to the top of the lighthouse. Fall was in full bloom with a vast array of trees boasting vivid colors of orange, crimson, and gold. They vowed to make a return trip to the festival each year from that day forward.

Jasmine found herself captivated by Kendall's calming voice. The trip sounded amazing, and she admitted to herself how physically attractive Kendall was. With his curly hair, blue eyes and rugged build, he was nothing short of gorgeous. She'd discerned he was a kind man, too, but still, she had no recollection.

"Kendall, I'm so sorry," she said, her expression blank. "I just don't remember."

He assured her it was okay. He'd keep visiting. He'd keep talking. He'd be patient.

• • •

Kendall had been patient. Six, long months passed, comprised of visits, therapy and doctors. He'd read to Jasmine, watered her plants, brought popcorn…and just talked. He wrote her several letters for her to read when alone, hoping to spark some recall. She'd started reading them, but eventually stopped, she'd told him, because it was too painful not to remember.

It was as if they were becoming new friends. Still, a sharp ache stung at Kendall's chest each time Jasmine's eyes filled with a familiar depth.

The overcast gloom of September's arrival matched that of Kendall's heart. Jasmine, finally at home in her apartment, began regaining a sense of normalcy as she assimilated herself back into a daily routine. She still had no recollections of their Victorian Weekend, which served as a stark reminder to Kendall of the doctor's words, which kept reverberating in his mind. Jasmine's memory may never recover. You should prepare yourself for that possibility.

His hope was wavering.

• • •

On a crisp October morning, Jasmine sat alone in her apartment. Opening Kendall's remaining letters, she began to read. Skimming his words, she smiled when he spoke of how a butterfly is proof one can go through darkness and still emerge as something beautiful. When he suggested if she doesn't have her old memories, they could make new ones, her eyes glistened.

As his words floated off the pages, she felt as if she'd known him for years. She knew him very well…didn't she?

One of the letters contained words describing a seaside Victorian resort with gas lamp-lit streets, and the phrase, "There's nothing like a Victorian Fall".

Her breath caught in her throat. Victorian Fall? Her eyes shut tight. Cape May.

• • •

He stood at the top of the lighthouse among the orange, red and plum-colored trees lining the bay below. Wearing his black tailcoat, complete with a floral vest and top hat, he shut his eyes against hot tears. Spontaneous sobs burst from his chest at the thought of a new reality without Jasmine.

Ascending footsteps sounded behind him. He swiped away the moisture from his cheeks as a familiar, sweet scent of vanilla perfume wafted through the air. He turned to discover the most beautiful woman he'd ever seen wearing a flowing yellow dress and a floppy, flower-lined hat.

Jasmine!

They held each other's gaze for a long moment before he finally spoke, "I don't understand. Why are you here? Do you…remember?"

Jasmine put her finger to his lips, smiling. Pulling his face closer, she pressed her lips against his, then whispered, "There's nothing like a Victorian Fall."

Acknowledgements

So many people to thank! Warm, heartfelt thanks to the following:

First and foremost, to you, my reader for choosing your valuable time to escape into my stories; I'm honored. To my family and friends for their continual nuggets of support and affirmation. To my dear friend, Marcia, for being like, the best cheerleader. To my writing tribe for nurturing my confidence and providing unparalleled encouragement. Finally, to my Jeffrey, who always believes in me and paves the way for me to follow my dreams.

Note from the Author

I sincerely hope you've enjoyed reading my stories as much as I've enjoyed writing them. Also, I hope you come back for more! To be the first to hear of any new publications please sign up for my mailing list at www.dawnvanbeck.com. Please be assured your email will never be shared, and you can unsubscribe at any time.

Hoping you will share your love of my stories with others... that's the best way for other readers to find my books! If you've enjoyed what you've read, please leave a review on the site for the store from which you purchased it. Your efforts and support are so greatly appreciated.

Feel free to connect with me on:

www.dawnvanbeck.com

Facebook Dawn Van Beck

Pinterest Dawn Van Beck

Twitter @dawnvanbeck

Happy Reading!

About the Author

Hi there! Welcome to “me”. I’m a writer, singer, child of God, and chocolate chip cookie connoisseur. I hold a degree in Human Resources with a concentration in Gerontology which has allowed me a rewarding career advocating for vulnerable senior adults. After transitioning out of my private Guardianship practice of several years, I now work alongside my husband with our moving business as well as put in some part-time hours at an Elder Law office... still advocating for seniors.

My love of all things writing began at an early age, pretending to be a librarian leading “story time” with my imaginary patrons. Over the years I’ve contributed to various publications including newsletters, magazines and theater pieces. My first official publication was in 1993 for the magazine “West Coast Woman”, where I shared my experience of living with a Multiple Sclerosis diagnosis. Now, after years of dreaming, I’m finally publishing the dozens of short stories I’ve written as well as a children’s picture book and working on wrapping up a Christian Romance novel.

I make my home in sunny Florida where I'm surrounded by a ridiculous number of writing journals and artisan coffee mugs. I love rummaging through antique shops, the arresting aroma of lavender, and I admit a quirky affinity for all things office supplies! Closer to my heart are bear hugs from my crazy husband, time spent with my adult children, and the companionship of Lilly, our feisty Daschund.

I believe we all have a voice and many things need to be said. What better way than to write stuff down? For me, writing is a way to express my thoughts of the world around me, to describe experiences that move my spirit, and to share how God meets me daily just as I am, with all my broken pieces. Join me as we journey together sharing short stories, devotions, miscellaneous musings and an occasional rant or two (or three).

Come, sit for a spell... I'll put the coffee on.

Books by Dawn Van Beck

Short Story Collections:
Autumn Love (Three Short & Sweet Romance Stories)
Holiday Moments (Holiday Short Stories) – *Coming Soon!*
More Coming in 2020!

Children's Picture Books:
Lazy Lilly and the Big Surprise – *Coming Soon!*

Christian Short Stories:
Child of Mine – *Coming Soon!*

Made in the USA
Columbia, SC
28 March 2023